A Fish Wish

Fay Robinson

Illustrated by Wayne Anderson

templar publishing

First published in the UK in 2005 by Templar Publishing.
This softback edition first published in the UK in 2006 by Templar Publising,
an imprint of The Templar Company plc,
Pippbrook Mill, London Road, Dorking, Surrey, RH4 1JE, UK
www.templarco.co.uk

Illustrations copyright © 2005 by Wayne Anderson
www.wayneandersonart.com
Text copyright © 2005 by Fay Robinson

First softback edition

ISBN-13: 978-1-84011-601-4
ISBN-10: 1-84011-601-3

Designed by Mike Jolley
Edited by Sue Harris

Printed in Hong Kong by Printing Express Ltd

For Emily, who knew what to do about the whale
F.R.

For Elizabeth Alice
W.A.

Elizabeth loved fish.

She spent every Saturday at the aquarium down the street, drawing her favourite ones. Everyone at the aquarium knew her. The aquarium librarian let her take out all the best books.

The fish feeder let Elizabeth give snails to the octopus. The plumber even let Elizabeth help clean the fish tanks.

At home, Elizabeth only had a guppy. She wished she had more fish.

"Mum, can I have a piranha?"

"No, Elizabeth, you may not have a banana. We're eating lunch in just a minute," said Elizabeth's mother.

"Mum, did you hear me? I said I want a piranha. It's a kind of fish. I already have a fish bowl for it."

Elizabeth kept several fish bowls on hand in the hope of using them someday.

"One fish is enough, Elizabeth. Maybe in a few years when you're more responsible."

"Hmph!" grumbled Elizabeth.

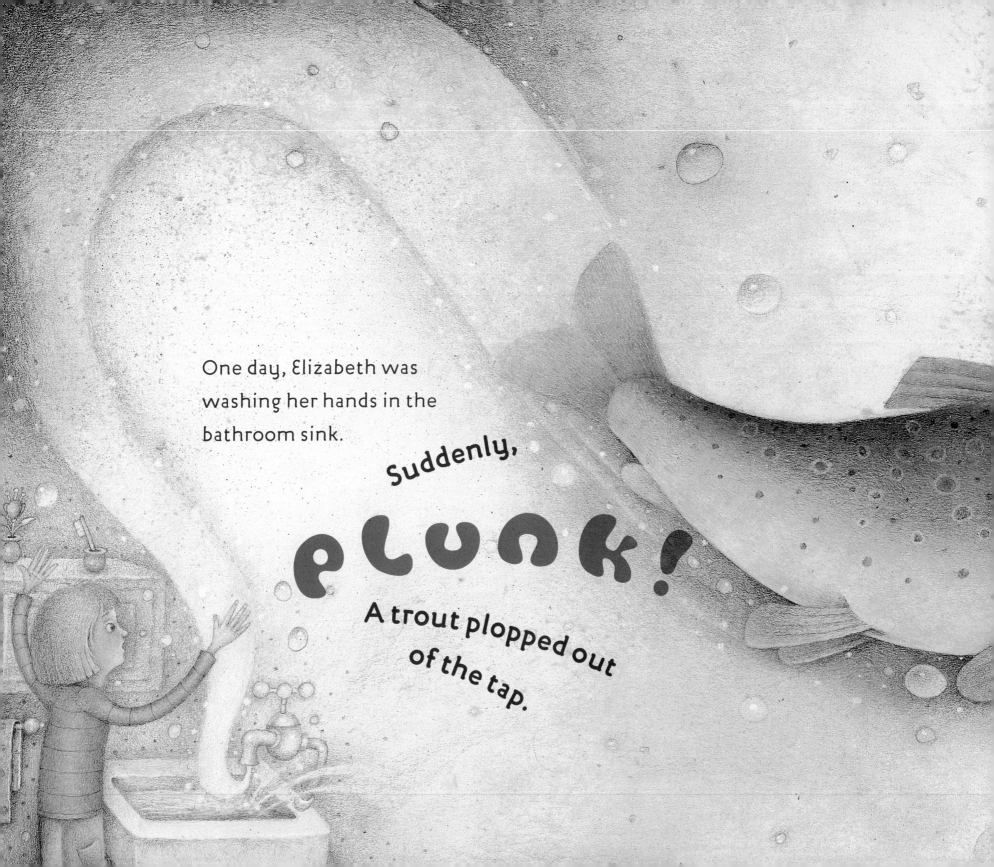

One day, Elizabeth was washing her hands in the bathroom sink.

Suddenly, **PLUNK!**

A trout plopped out of the tap.

"Terrific!" said Elizabeth.
She ran to get one of her fish bowls.

"Mum!" Elizabeth called. **"Look! A trout!"**

"Yes, dear," said her mother.
But she wasn't really listening.

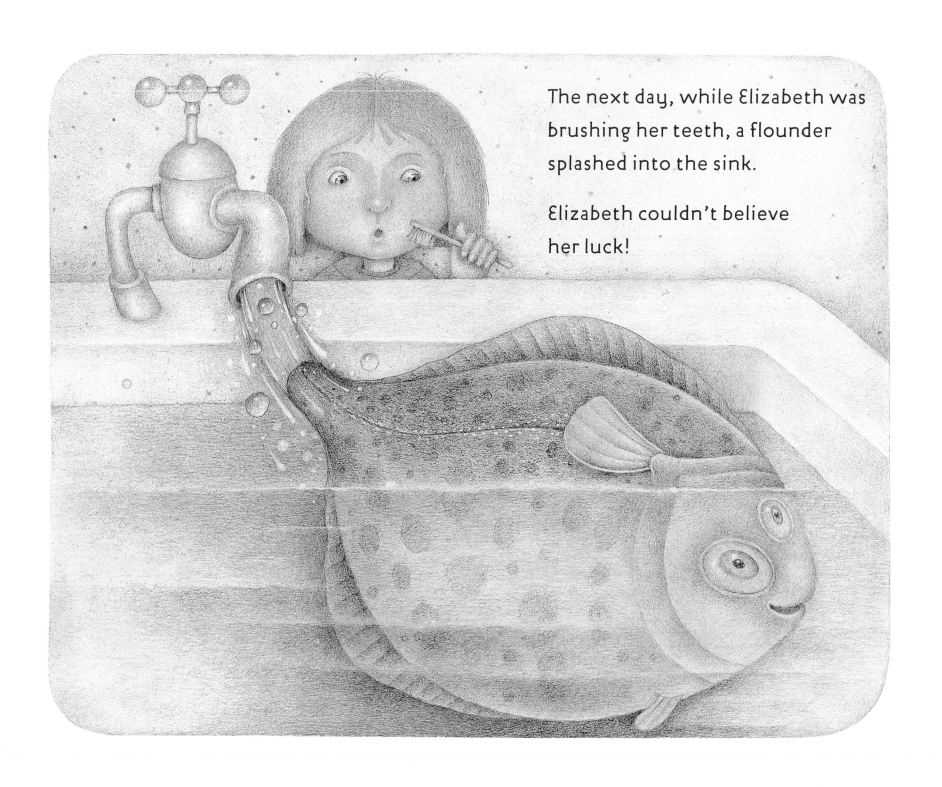

The next day, while Elizabeth was brushing her teeth, a flounder splashed into the sink.

Elizabeth couldn't believe her luck!

"Dad," said Elizabeth,
"why do flounders have both eyes
on the same side?"

"Elizabeth, show me your project later.
I'm busy now," said Elizabeth's father.

"Nobody **ever** listens to me,"
said Elizabeth.

Elizabeth turned the water on again. Just as she expected, another fish appeared.

This one was a little larger than the others and didn't quite fit into any of her fish bowls.

Elizabeth gathered up all the pocket money she had been saving and hurried to the pet shop. She bought three large fish tanks and hauled them home.

The **next** day,
a moray eel oozed out of the tap.
A clown triggerfish followed.
Then a squid showed up.

Soon there were tanks full of fish
on every shelf and in every corner—
catfish, dogfish, jellyfish, and rays;
sticklebacks, halibut,
lumpfish, skates...

swishing, zipping, and **splashing** with delight.

Elizabeth's parents hadn't noticed.

Elizabeth thought she should bring it to their attention.

"I just love having all these fish around," she said at dinner.

"That's nice, dear. Please pass the pepper," said her mother.

Elizabeth tried again. "My favourite fish so far is the sea dragon. Look, it's watching us!"

"Personally, my favourite dish is lasagne. Maybe I'll make one tomorrow," said her father.

After dinner, Elizabeth decided to take a bath. She turned on the taps and a giant mouth appeared. Elizabeth jumped back and waited while the creature finished squishing through the pipes.

Soon a baby beluga whale **splashed** into the tub.

Elizabeth sighed. "There's no room for any more fish, much less a whale," she said.

"It's time to make my parents listen."

She hurried downstairs.

"Mum, Dad, I've got a problem," Elizabeth said.

"Don't worry, dear," said her mother. "Most children think they have problems."

"No, really. Listen to me," said Elizabeth. "There are fish coming out of the taps in the bathroom."

"When I was a child, I thought there were snakes behind the walls," said Elizabeth's father.

"But there really **are** fish," said Elizabeth. "Don't you **see** them?"

Before her parents could respond...

a rumble from above interrupted them.

"What's that?" said Elizabeth's father, looking up.

The ceiling tiles shook and clacked. A trickle of water dribbled onto the kitchen table.

"Is it raining?"

asked Elizabeth's mother.

A clanging, banging sound came next.
The trickle became a small waterfall.

Ceiling tiles clattered to the floor.
The noise grew thunderous.
   "I think we should get out of the way,"
called Elizabeth, pulling her parents to the side.

**Suddenly, the ceiling split open as something
huge and grey came** whooshing down.

The beluga whale looked sweetly at Elizabeth's mother from the tub.

"Elizabeth, can you e-e-explain this f-f-fish?" asked Elizabeth's mother.

"It's a beluga whale, Mum."

"Yes, honey, but what's it doing here in our kitchen?"

"It came out of the tap. It must have been too heavy for the bathroom floor. There are lots of others."

"I've been **trying** to tell you."

"I'll call the fire brigade!" said Elizabeth's mother.

"And I'll call the police!" said Elizabeth's father.

Elizabeth patted the whale on the head. "I'll call the plumber from the aquarium. He'll know what to do," she said.

The plumber arrived and got right to work.

"Oh dear...

looks to me like you've got yourself a fish jam,"
he said. "Yep. A traffic jam of fish. Happens when the
aquarium pipes cross with peoples' plumbing.

It's a lot more common than you'd think."

"Wha, wha, wha...?" said Elizabeth's mother.
"They don't like being stuck in a pipe
any more than you would," he explained.

"The only thing to do
is to turn on all the taps and **let 'em out!**"

Elizabeth and the plumber shut all the windows and turned on all the taps.
Then they led everyone outside.

The house filled up with water.

Soon there were fish peering out from every window.

"Might as well turn your house into an aquarium," said the plumber with a wink. "Can't live in it now."

Elizabeth shouted, **"Yes!"**

Her wish for fish had come true!

Her parents gasped.

Elizabeth and her family moved to a house nearby.
Elizabeth's old house became a home for wayward
fish. Elizabeth took excellent care of them.

And from then on,
Elizabeth's parents listened **very carefully**
whenever Elizabeth spoke.

Especially when she mentioned a new hobby....

New Aquarium
open

The End...?